RUSS THOMPSON

TORN

Finding Forward

Books

Published by Finding Forward Books
P.O. Box 8182, Long Beach, CA 90808
www.findingforwardbooks.com

Editing by Laura Perkins. Series concept by Pam Sheppard. Text set in Open Dyslexic Mono.

LCCN: 2022909303
ISBN: 978-1-7373157-5-9
FILE: FF007-22F-2024-07-25

Summary: Perry Fletcher is a straight-A student in his senior year of high school. He has a chance to win a track scholarship. But he wrecks his knee chasing a thief who steals a package from his porch. What happens when the thief becomes one of his classmates?

BISAC Subject Codes: YOUNG ADULT FICTION / Social Themes / Poverty and Homelessness | YOUNG ADULT FICTION / Sports and Recreation / Track and Field | YOUNG ADULT FICTION / Social Themes / Emotions and Feelings

Lexile measure: HL400L

For Betty Jean,
our kids,
and grandkids.

CONTENTS

1 WHAT IF?

SATURDAY AFTERNOON. It's nice to have the house to myself.

And it's raining, so I don't have to mow the yard.

I take a bite out of my sandwich and look out the kitchen window.

A delivery guy pulls up and brings a box to our door.

I should get it now. But I want to finish my sandwich first.

Minutes pass. A white car with a dent in the side pulls up.

A little kid with red hair gets

out and hurries up our walk.

Something doesn't seem right.

I look again. He's running away.

I rush out the door to catch him.

My foot slips on the sidewalk.

Something inside my knee pops.

I fall and hit the ground.

LATER. I look out the kitchen
window.

Mom pulls into the driveway with
Olive sitting next to her.

They're home from the market. I
go out to help bring in the
groceries.

"Perry, how come you're limping?"
Olive asks.

I can't say what really happened.
I promised Mom I would watch
carefully for the package and bring
it in right away.

"I slipped in some water on the kitchen floor," I say. "It feels like I twisted my knee."

"Let me take a look at it when we get inside," Mom says. "Did the package come?"

"Not yet."

We walk into the house.

I feel bad about lying.

DINNER. I sit at the kitchen table with Mom and Olive.

Mom made tacos, which I love.

But my knee is killing me. I thought it would be better by now.

"Perry, I checked on the package," Mom says. "The website shows it was delivered. Are you sure you didn't see anything?"

"No, there was nothing."

"Maybe we got porched," Olive

says.

"I don't think so," I say. "I was watching for it all afternoon."

"Maybe it will show up tomorrow," Mom says. "I ordered books to give to the kids in my seventh-grade English classes."

I feel bad about lying again.

EVENING. I sit at the kitchen table and work on my calculus.

I try to concentrate. But it's hard.

My knee is freezing because of the ice bag I have on it.

I get on School View and check my grades again. It feels good to look at all my A's.

But it's my senior year, my last year to run track at Edison High School.

Everything has been perfect until today.

What if my knee doesn't get better?

2 COLD

MONDAY MORNING. Olive and I ride in the car with Mom.

It's raining again, so she's taking us to school. The spring semester starts today.

"Olive, do you have any new classes?" I ask.

"They're all the same," she says. "But I have a new teacher in history. What about you?"

"I have peer tutoring this semester instead of peer counseling."

"What's peer tutoring?" she asks.

"We help kids with their homework when they come to study hall. It should be pretty easy."

Mom drops us off in front of Edison High School. We walk through the front gate.

I try not to limp. But my knee still hurts from Saturday.

It's noisy with everybody talking and laughing. I look for Hector and Vincent. But I don't see them.

Olive turns to go to the tenth-grade lockers.

She's still my little sister. But she's older now.

It probably won't be long before she has a boyfriend.

A.P. ENGLISH. Mr. Zimmer comes to the front of the classroom.

"Open up your books to page 128,"
he says. "We have to move quickly.
There are only 67 school days before
the Advanced Placement test."

Things are happening fast.

In April I'll find out which
colleges accepted me. In September,
I'll be in college.

My first choice is Munson State.
They have a great track program.

Also, it's a hundred miles away.
If I go to Munson, I'll get to live
in a dorm.

Raymond State is my second
choice. It's also good.

But it's only five miles away. If
I go to Raymond, I'll be living at
home.

PEER TUTORING. We meet with Mr.
Rubio in his classroom before going

to the study hall.

There are sixteen peer tutors.
All of us are seniors.

"The work you will be doing is
important," he says. "The students
you'll be working with got NoPasses
in at least two classes last
semester. Our goal is for them to
get C's or higher in everything by
the end of the school year. You can
change their lives by helping them."

He says that stuff a lot. But for
me, the main thing is that it will
be an easy A.

"Most of them will need help in
math," he says. "Even if math is not
your favorite subject, you will
still need to help them with it."

We leave Mr. Rubio's classroom
and go to the study hall. It's a big
room with about forty tables.

Mr. Rubio looks at his list and calls out the table numbers.

I go to table six and shake hands with the guy. He seems okay.

I look sideways. Something seems familiar about the kid sitting at the next table.

He's a little guy with red hair and freckles.

I look at him again.

Then it hits me.

He's the kid who porched us.

Mr. Rubio calls roll. The guy's name is Doyle.

It makes me mad to look at him.

LUNCH. It's still raining. The food court is dry. But it's cold because the wind blows through.

Hector and Vincent are already at our table. I sit down across from them and take out my sandwich.

"Perry, do you want to run to the train bridge today?" Hector asks.

My knee still hurts. I probably shouldn't run.

But maybe it will be okay after I get it warmed up.

"Sure," I say. "Sounds good."

The wind blows harder. I zip up my jacket and look around the food court.

That's when I see him.

Doyle sits off to the side with some other guys.

The wind blows harder.

He doesn't have a jacket, just his school uniform shirt.

It makes me feel cold to look at him.

3 HAVE TO

AFTER SCHOOL. I try to run with
Hector and Vincent down Orchard
Street.

I should be ahead of them. But my
knee hurts worse than it did
yesterday.

They stop at a red light. I catch
up to them.

"Perry, are you sure you should
be running on that thing?" Hector
asks.

"I'll be okay. It's starting to
feel better."

The light turns green. We run along Saturn Street next to the train tracks.

The pain gets worse.

They pull ahead.

I'm a block behind them.

Hector and Vincent get to another red light and turn to look at me.

I wave and signal that I'm going back to Edison.

I was league champion in the 3200 meters last year.

This year, I have a chance to go to the state track finals.

But if my knee doesn't get better, there will be nothing.

HOME. I sit at the kitchen table with a bag of ice on my knee.

Mom is gone because she's taking a night class at Raymond State.

Olive cooks dinner. She's making stir-fry tonight.

I look at my knee. It hurts because of that kid in peer tutoring.

"Olive, do you know a guy named Doyle?" I ask.

"What does he look like?"

"Short and skinny, with red hair and freckles."

"I have him in math," she says. "What about him?"

"He's in peer tutoring. I think he's a bad guy."

"What do you mean?" she asks. "He seems nice to me."

"Just be careful. I know some things about him. He may seem nice on the outside. But on the inside, he's messed up."

Olive acts like she doesn't care

what I say.

It makes me mad to think of him.

He needs to get arrested.

EVENING. I sit at the kitchen table
and work on my calculus.

Mom's phone rings. "Hi honey,"
she says.

It's Dad making his nightly video
call. His truck stop tonight is in
Lupton, Arizona.

Mom talks to him first. Next,
it's Olive's turn.

Finally, it's my turn.

I'm always glad to see him. But
he looks so lonely. That's why I
would never want to be a truck
driver.

"Perry, how's your knee doing?"
he asks.

"I tried to run on it today. But

the pain got worse and I had to give
it up."

"You were smart to do that," he
says.

"Thanks. But track practice
starts next week."

"You have to let it heal," Dad
says. "We had a guy when I went to
Munson who messed up his ankle. But
he tried to come back too soon.
Because of that, he had to get
surgery."

I know he's right.

But I have to start running soon.

4 BECAUSE OF HIM

TUESDAY MORNING. The alarm goes off. The pain in my knee hits me.

I sit up in bed and push my finger on the swelling.

The skin is puffy, like there's water underneath.

I limp to the kitchen for breakfast. Mom and Olive are already there.

"Perry, is it feeling any better?" Mom asks.

"I think it's worse. It feels like things are squishing and

crunching inside."

"I'll take you to school this morning so you don't have to walk," Mom says. "If it still feels bad this afternoon, I'll take you to urgent care."

We finish breakfast. I go back to my room to get dressed.

It hurts to bend my knee when I put my pants on.

A.P. ENGLISH. The bell rings to begin class.

Mr. Zimmer comes to the front of the room. He clicks on his computer and puts a test question on the screen.

"This is an essay question like those you will have on the Advanced Placement test," he says. "Remember to relax, get to the point quickly,

and write clearly. You will have
forty minutes."

I begin the test.

Writing is usually easy for me.

But it's hard to concentrate
because of my knee.

PEER TUTORING. Mr. Rubio comes to
the front of the study hall.

He says nothing but looks at each
of us.

"One of the things I want all of
you to know, is that you can all be
successful here," he says. "And if
you're successful in high school,
you'll be ready for college."

I've heard him say this a million
times. But he really means what he
says.

"There are people who think that
college is only for some students,"

he says. "But it's not. College is for everybody."

I look sideways at Doyle. His eyes are glued on Mr. Rubio.

There's a book in front of him, *I Survived Hurricane Katrina.*

It's one of Mom's books that he stole.

I want to grab it.

But I don't want to make a scene.

LOCKER ROOM. Period six. Coach Quinty stands near the door to the weight room.

"Perry, you look like you're limping pretty bad," he says.

"It's going to be okay. I just twisted it a little bit."

"Have you seen a doctor?" he asks.

"Not yet."

"I know how bad you want to run," he says. "But don't be like me. I threw away my chance to play pro football because I messed up my knee and kept playing on it."

I think about Doyle again. All of this is because of him.

5 DON'T SAY

THREE DAYS LATER. Mom and I wait in one of the exam rooms at Dr. Thurman's office.

My knee has gotten worse. I get sharp pains every time I put weight on it.

There's a knock on the door. Dr. Thurman comes in.

She's old, probably about fifty. She walks with a cane, which worries me.

If her leg is messed up, how can she fix mine?

"Perry, the MRI was very clear," she says. "You have a torn medial meniscus."

"What does that mean?" I ask.

"The meniscus is the pad between the bones in your knee. If it tears, it causes pain and swelling. You might get a grinding or squishing feeling in your knee when you walk. You can also lose your range of motion."

"I'm having all of that."

"Do you remember how it felt when you hurt it?" she asks.

"There was a pop inside."

"That was your meniscus tearing," she says. "Sometimes it can heal on its own. If it doesn't, the next option is surgery."

"What about track?"

"You'll be out for at least a

month," she says. "If you try to run
before it's healed, you'll do more
damage. I'm writing you a
prescription to get medication for
the swelling. You also need to get
crutches."

I like Dr. Thurman. But I don't
care what she says. There is no way
I'm going to use crutches.

I'm going to get back to running.

I'm going to make it to the state
track finals.

And I'm going to get a
scholarship to Munson State.

EVENING. I sit at the kitchen table
and work on my calculus.

Mom's phone rings. It's Dad with
his video call.

"How was it with the doctor?" he
asks me.

"She gave me some pills and said
I have to use crutches."

"That's a good idea," he says.
"Do exactly what she says. The more
you stay off your knee, the quicker
it will heal."

He thinks he's right.

But my knee is starting to feel
better.

And I don't need crutches.

LATER. I'm almost in bed when Mom
knocks on my door.

She comes in with a set of
crutches.

They're the old wooden ones that
have been hanging in the garage.
Grandpa used them when he was a kid.

"I know you don't want these,"
she says. "But your knee won't get
better if you don't do what the

doctor says. You have to use them."

I don't feel like getting into an argument.

I look away and don't say anything.

6 MAYBE I CAN

MONDAY MORNING. Mom drives Olive and me to school.

My knee feels better. But Mom is making sure I don't walk.

I look at my crutches.

They make me mad.

I'm not a cripple.

We get to school. Mom pulls to the curb.

"Perry, are you sure you're going to be okay?" she asks.

"I'll be fine," I say. "My knee is feeling better."

Olive and I get out of the car and go through the front gate. It's early, so nobody else is around yet.

I go to the bushes by the science building, hide my crutches, and walk to the food court.

My knee is healing faster than Dr. Thurman said it would.

LUNCH. I sit across the table from Hector and Vincent.

"Perry, you look like you're walking better," Hector says. "What did the doctor say?"

"It's not that bad. I just have to take it easy for a while."

"What about track?" Vincent asks.

"I talked to Coach Quinty. I'm going to lift weights and ride on the exercise bike."

"It sounds boring," Vincent says.

I take a bite out of my sandwich. "You got that right."

TRACK PRACTICE. I finish stretching with the team, go to the weight room, and start pedaling on the exercise bike.

My knee hurts at first.

But after I warm up, it feels better.

Maybe I can start running in two weeks instead of four.

7   KEEP GOING

TUESDAY, LUNCH. I get to our table and sit across from Hector and Vincent.

"How was practice yesterday?" I ask.

"You're lucky you weren't out there," Hector says. "We ran a bunch of four-hundreds. Coach Quinty was trying to kill us."

"How many did you do?" I ask.

"I don't know," Vincent says. "But we had to do them all at full speed. And when some of the guys dropped back, he made us do more."

I wish I could have been there with them.

AFTER SCHOOL. Weight room. I get off the exercise bike.

It's been ten days since I hurt my knee. But finally, it's starting to feel better.

I leave the weight room and walk to the dirt path that goes around the baseball field.

It's perfect. Coach Quinty won't be able to see me here.

I take a few steps.

My knee feels okay.

I begin jogging.

I feel twinges.

I slow down and walk.

The twinges go away.

I jog again.

My knee feels better.

Dr. Thurman will be surprised that I was able to start running so soon.

HOME. I sit at the kitchen table with a bag of ice on my knee.

I try to do my calculus. But it's hard to think because the ice is so cold.

Olive comes in and sits across from me.

"Perry, I heard you were running around the baseball field," she says. "The doctor told you not to run."

"I wasn't running. I was jogging. And my knee doesn't hurt. It's just swollen."

"You're being stupid," Olive says.

"No, I'm not. You don't know what you're talking about."

I'm glad when she leaves.

I'm not going to quit.

I don't care what she or anybody else says.

I'm going to work through the pain and keep going.

8 SEEN IT BEFORE

WEDNESDAY. A.P. English. There's a knock on the door.

Coach Quinty steps into the room, whispers something to Mr. Zimmer, and signals for me to step outside.

I follow him into the hall.

"Perry, what were you doing after school yesterday?" he asks.

"Jogging around the baseball field."

"What were you supposed to be doing?"

"I was riding on the exercise

bike. But my knee felt good, so I thought I would try jogging a little."

"What did the doctor tell you?"

"She said to wait."

"Perry, your knee is no joke," Coach Quinty says. "You have a great future. Don't throw it away by not listening to your doctor. No running until I get a note from your mom."

He thinks he knows. But he doesn't know.

My knee is not his knee.

PEER TUTORING. I walk through the door of the study hall.

Doyle is already there.

He has a new book on the table in front of him, *I Survived the California Wildfires*.

It's another one of Mom's books

that he stole.

I feel like smacking him.

But I don't want to get suspended.

LUNCH. Hector and Vincent are already at our table when I get there.

I sit down and take out my sandwich.

"What was practice like yesterday?" I ask.

"Not good," Vincent says. "Coach Quinty was trying to kill us again."

I look past them. I can't believe what I see.

Olive is walking with Doyle.

I look closer.

She's holding his hand.

"Perry, what's wrong?" Hector asks.

"Nothing," I say. "It's just
something I have to deal with."

I feel like I'm going to explode.

AFTER SCHOOL. I walk to Addison
Park.

It has a good jogging trail. And
it's the best place for me to run so
Coach Quinty won't find out.

I reach the trail and begin
jogging.

My knee feels pretty good.

I speed up.

I feel twinges.

I slow down.

The twinges go away.

I keep jogging and see the
parking lot.

The section by the restrooms has
cars and vans with people living in
them.

There's an old white car with a
dent in the side.

It seems like I've seen it
before.

9 STRAIGHT AHEAD

THURSDAY MORNING. It's nice to be off my crutches. I walk to school with Olive.

My knee only has a little pain.

But I'm still mad at Doyle.

And I can't stand that Olive was holding hands with him yesterday.

I don't want to lose my temper. But I have to say something.

"Olive, what's going on? I saw you holding hands with that Doyle kid."

"What do you mean by that?" she

asks.

"I told you to stay away from him."

"Maybe you don't know what you're talking about," she says. "Maybe I think he's a nice guy."

She runs ahead.

There's no way I can catch up to her with my knee messed up.

I have to get her away from him.

PEER TUTORING. I sit at my normal table and wait to begin. Mr. Rubio comes to the front.

"I'm changing tutoring partners today based on your test scores from last week," he says. "If you're a tutor, I will call out the number of your new table."

He begins calling out names and numbers.

"Perry," he says. "Table seven."

He matched me up with Doyle.

I pretend not to hear.

Mr. Rubio calls my name again and
looks at me.

I have no choice. I move to table
seven and sit across from Doyle.

He reaches out to give me a fist
bump.

I pretend not to notice and keep
my hand down.

"Should I start?" he asks.

"Go ahead," I say. "I'll watch as
you work."

He opens his math book and tries
to do a problem.

He writes down a bunch of
numbers. But he has no idea what to
do with them.

I ask him to read the problem out
loud.

He looks at the page but doesn't say anything.

I wonder if he knows all the words.

I read the problem to him and show him how to solve it.

It takes him a while, but he gets it.

A smile appears on his face.

"Thanks," he says. "You're helping me."

He seems like he wants to learn.

But he stole from our porch.

AFTER SCHOOL. Addison Park. I reach the jogging trail and begin running.

My knee feels better. It won't be long until I'm back to full speed again.

I get to the parking lot and see the same old cars and vans that I saw yesterday.

The white car is also there. The back seat is piled high with stuff.

A lady sits in the front with her head back.

A kid with a red hair sits next to her.

It looks like they might be living there.

The kid turns his head.

It's Doyle.

I look straight ahead and keep running.

10 HAVE TO

FRIDAY MORNING. Olive and I walk to school.

She usually talks the whole time.

But today she's giving me the silent treatment. It's because of what I said about Doyle yesterday.

I wish I had kept my mouth shut.

I feel differently now.

It's not his fault that he's homeless.

And it's probably his mom who was making him steal.

PEER TUTORING. I sit next to Doyle. His math test is in front of him.

It has NoPass written at the top.

"Perry, you may not think so," he says. "But I really am trying."

"I know you are," I say. "We're going to work on it."

I feel bad about the grade he got.

And I feel bad because he's homeless.

But you would never know by looking at him that he lives in a car.

He smiles. His clothes are always clean. And he seems like anybody else.

"Have you talked to your math teacher?" I ask.

"It's Mr. Braden," he says. "He only cares about the smart kids.

He'll tell me it's my own fault for
not listening."

Doyle is right. I have Mr. Braden
for calculus. He says things like
that all the time.

"I know it's hard," I say. "But
you have to keep trying. I'll help
you as much as I can."

I watch as Doyle begins working.
He's trying hard.
I can tell he wants to learn.

LUNCH. I open my backpack and take
out my sandwich. Hector and Vincent
sit across from me.

"How did it go with running at
the park yesterday?" Hector asks.

"Pretty good," I say. "My knee is
feeling better."

"Do you know you're still
limping?" Vincent asks.

It surprises me to hear him say that. I thought I was walking fine.

I look to the side and see Olive holding hands with Doyle.

Both of them are smiling.

Maybe it will be okay.

AFTER SCHOOL. Locker room. I take a deep breath and knock on the door of the P.E. office.

Coach Quinty motions for me to come inside.

I give him the note I forged.

"This is from my mom," I say. "It's okay for me to start running again."

He looks at the note and frowns. "What did the doctor say?"

"She said it's okay. I just have to stop running if I feel any pain."

"I still think you need to wait,"

Coach Quinty says. "But it's your mom's decision."

I leave the office.

I feel bad about forging the note.

But Munson State is slipping away from me.

I have to get back to running.

11 BUT SHE DOESN'T

MONDAY AFTERNOON. Track practice. It feels good to be back with the team again.

I sit on the grass for stretching next to Hector and Vincent.

"Perry, how's your knee?" Hector asks.

"Feeling better. It's not as bad as the doctor thought it was."

We finish stretching and start running four-hundreds.

My knee hurts when I go around the turns. But it doesn't slow me down.

I also have pain during the rest of the workout. But not as much as yesterday.

Dad told me that sometimes you have to put the pain out of your mind and work through it.

I think he would be proud of me.

HOME. I sit on the couch with an ice bag on my knee.

I knew it would be swollen. But I didn't think it would be this bad.

"Perry, your knee doesn't look so good," Olive says.

"It's fine," I say. "This ice is just to keep it from swelling."

"If it's fine, why were you limping when you got home?"

"I wasn't limping. I was just walking slow because we had a hard practice."

I can tell by the look on her
face that she doesn't believe me.

But I don't care.

It's my knee.

I know what I'm doing.

AFTER DINNER. Olive and I clean up
the kitchen.

Mom sits in the living room. Her
phone rings.

"Hi, Coach Quinty," she says.
"What happened?... He brought you a
what?... I haven't talked to the
doctor since last week... Thanks for
calling. I'll talk to him tonight."

I should have known he would
call. What was I thinking?

LATER. I sit at the kitchen table
doing homework.

Mom comes in and sits across from me. I know I'm in trouble.

"Coach Quinty said you forged a note from me," she says.

"My knee feels like it's getting better. I thought it would be okay to start running."

"I've been watching the way you walk," she says. "And it doesn't look better to me. Also, you lied."

"If I don't start running again, there's no way I can make it to the state track finals."

"What if you make your knee worse?" she asks. "What if you do permanent damage?"

"That won't happen. I know what I'm doing."

"You're fooling yourself because you want to run," she says. "I'm grounding you for lying and forging that note. Don't make a mistake that you'll regret for the rest of your life."

I don't care if I'm grounded.

I'm glad when she leaves.

My knee is getting better.

She thinks she knows what she's talking about.

But she doesn't.

12 BEATEN

TUESDAY MORNING. Peer tutoring. Doyle is happy. I've never seen him like this before.

"Perry, I got a C on my math test," he says. "Mr. Braden shook my hand and everything."

It feels good to hear him say that.

But it also makes me think.

I have almost everything.

Doyle has almost nothing.

And he's the one who's happy.

"Can you help me with my

history?" he asks. "I have a report due tomorrow."

He shows me the rough draft he wrote. The ideas are good. But the grammar and spelling need work.

I show him what to do. Forty minutes later, he's done.

"It's funny," he says. "I've always wanted to run track. But I couldn't because of my grades. Maybe I can now."

It's too late for him to join the track team because he messed up on the last report card.

But I don't have the heart to tell him.

THE BELL RINGS. Peer tutoring ends. I go into the hall and begin walking to third period.

There's a tap on my shoulder.

It's Doyle.

"Is this yours?" he asks. "I found it under your chair."

He holds out my cell phone. It must have fallen out of my pocket.

He could have kept it and sold it.

I never would have known.

AFTER SCHOOL. I can't run with the track team.

But I'm not going to let that stop me.

I finish my workout in the weight room, leave campus, and walk to Addison Park.

It feels good to run on the jogging trail.

Next year at this time I'll be living in a dorm, running on the Munson State track team, and majoring in computer science.

The parking lot is ahead. I turn
right to stay away from it.

I don't want Doyle to see me.

He would never want me to know
that he's homeless.

FORTY MINUTES LATER. I leave the
park and begin walking home.

Two police cars drive by with
their red lights flashing.

The car they pull over looks like
Doyle's car.

I get closer. It is.

Doyle and his mom get out.

The police put handcuffs on them.

Doyle looks straight at me.

I can see the beaten look in his
eyes.

13 NO IDEA

WEDNESDAY MORNING. Peer tutoring.
Doyle is here.

I'm relieved to see him.

But he stares straight ahead when
I get to our table.

"What happened?" I ask.

"I don't want to talk about it."

He leans forward and puts his
head down.

I wish I knew what to say.

AFTER SCHOOL. Addison Park. I begin
running.

I wait for the pain in my knee to stop.

But it doesn't.

There's a bench next to the jogging trail.

I sit down and look at my knee.

The swelling is worse.

I should have listened to Dr. Thurman.

HOME. I open the front door. Mom is cooking dinner.

"Perry, how was school?"

"Not bad. Just a regular day."

"Your limping is worse," she says. "Let me see your knee."

I sit down and pull up my pant leg.

The swelling looks like there's a water balloon inside.

Mom frowns. "Are you sure you

didn't run today?"

"I didn't run at all. I only walked to my classes."

I'm tired of lying. But I can't tell her what I really did.

I hope I didn't do permanent damage.

AFTER DINNER. I sit at the kitchen table and try to do homework.

But I can't. I keep thinking about Doyle.

I get on my laptop and go to the *Conroy Courier*.

I find what I'm looking for under local news.

Suspected Porch Pirates Arrested

Conroy Police arrested a woman and an unidentified juvenile in a sting operation connected with a series of residential package thefts.

Irene Kemp, 38, was charged with grand theft, receiving stolen property, possession of methamphetamine, and child endangerment. She is being held at the Vernon County Jail.

The juvenile, age 15, was also charged.

Their vehicle was stopped by Conroy Police after a tracking device placed in a decoy package was activated.

Additional items reported stolen were also found in the vehicle.

LATER. I sit in the kitchen doing calculus. Olive comes in and sits across from me.

"Perry, did you hear what
happened to Doyle?" she asks.

"What?"

"He was arrested with his mom for
stealing packages off people's
porches. He got sent to a foster
home. His mom is in jail."

I feel bad for Olive. I can tell
she's broken up.

"His mom was making him do it,"
Olive says. "She got fired from her
job. Then they got evicted from
their apartment."

I remember when I chased Doyle.

I had no idea what he was going
through.

14 SHAKE HANDS

THURSDAY MORNING. Olive and I ride to school with Mom.

I sit in the front seat and look at my crutches.

The pain in my knee is not as bad as it was yesterday.

But I have to use them. Mom wouldn't give me a choice.

"Perry, I'll try to make an appointment for you to see Dr. Thurman this afternoon," Mom says.

"My knee isn't that bad. It will probably be okay if I just rest it."

"No, it won't," Mom says. "You need to get it looked at."

I know she's right. But I don't want to admit it.

Mom stops the car in front of school.

Olive and I get out.

I stand on my crutches.

It feels like track season is over for me.

PEER TUTORING. Doyle is already there when I get to our table.

He seems normal, not falling apart like he was yesterday.

"Perry, what's with the crutches?" he asks.

"I tried to run yesterday. But I hurt my knee again."

"What do you mean?"

"I run the 3200 meters on the

track team. But I messed up my knee.
I was hoping to make it to the state
finals this year."

"That's a drag," he says.

He probably still doesn't want to
talk. But I need to find out.

"Doyle, did things get any better
after that thing with the police?" I
ask.

"It's a long story," he says.

"You don't know this," I say.
"But I'm Olive's brother. She told
me what you said to her."

He looks mad at first. Then his
face relaxes.

I'm not sure I should ask. But I
can't keep it in. "Do you remember
two weeks ago on Saturday?"

"What do you mean?"

"We live in a gray house on
Gilbert Street. I was looking out

the window when you snatched a
package off our porch."

His face turns red.

"I ran after you. But I slipped
on the sidewalk. That's how I messed
up my knee."

He looks down at the table. I
wonder what's going through his
mind.

"I'm sorry," he says.

I can tell he really means it.

We look each other in the eye and
shake hands.

15 NO CHANCE

AFTERNOON. Mom and I sit in the waiting room at Dr. Thurman's office.

The nurse comes out and takes us to an exam room.

I hate walking on my crutches. But now I need to.

I sit on top of the exam table and move my legs.

My right knee feels perfect.

But my left knee feels like it's torn up inside.

"I hope you don't have permanent

damage," Mom says. "But Dr. Thurman told you what would happen if you ran on it."

I know what the doctor said. And I know I messed up by not listening to her. But I thought my knee was getting better.

There's a knock on the door. Dr. Thurman comes in. She frowns when she sees my knee.

"Perry, were you running on it?" she asks.

"It was feeling better. I thought it would be okay to run a little."

She shakes her head. "The news isn't good. Based on the swelling and what I can see on the MRI, the tearing has become worse. There could also be some other damage."

"You have a decision to make," Dr. Thurman says. "If I operate now,

the chances for a full recovery are
good. You should be running next
year. If I don't operate, you could
recover. But I'm not sure how well
you will be running."

I thought I could push through
the pain and it would be okay.

But instead, I made it worse.

Everything I've worked for is
being taken away from me.

SIX-THIRTY. We're almost home. Mom
pulls into the drive-through lane at
Burger House.

Normally, I would be happy about
getting food there.

But I can't stop thinking about
my knee.

I don't want surgery. But I also
want to run next year.

Mom said it should be my

decision.

I have a lot to think about.

LATER. There's a plastic shopping bag hanging on our doorknob when we get home.

Mom opens the bag. It's full of books.

"This is strange," she says. "These are the books I ordered two weeks ago. But they've all been used."

I look in the bag. They're the books Doyle stole.

I didn't want to tell Mom what happened.

But it's time.

"Remember the delivery that was supposed to come two weeks ago, the books?" I ask.

"What about it?"

"The package was delivered," I
say. "But I didn't pick it up right
away. A kid stole it off our porch.
I chased him. But I slipped on the
sidewalk. That's how I hurt my
knee."

"Why didn't you tell me in the
first place?" she asks.

"I felt bad because it was my
fault the books were stolen. The kid
who took them is a guy that I work
with in peer tutoring. We talked
about what happened. I guess he
decided to bring them back."

"Did he say whether he likes the
books?" Mom asks.

"I'm pretty sure he does. He's
been reading them at school."

Mom goes into her office and
brings out five more books.

"Take these to Doyle tomorrow,"

she says. "Tell him that I want him
to read them. That's what I bought
them for."

AFTER DINNER. Olive and I sit at the
kitchen table.
     She's doing homework.
     I look at medical websites to
find out about knee surgeries.
     Mom's phone rings.
     It's our video call from Dad. She
brings the phone into the kitchen.
     "Perry, I'm sorry about your
knee," he says. "Do you know what
you're going to do?"
     "I've been thinking about it a
lot. I've decided to get the
surgery."
     "I know it will be hard," he
says. "But I think you're doing the
right thing. Next year, you should

be fine."

I look away from the phone.

It's not fine.

Track season is over for me.

And there's no chance I'll be getting a track scholarship to Munson State.

16 NEED TO THINK

FRIDAY MORNING. Edison High School.
It's another rainy day.

Mom pulls up to the curb.

"Perry, be careful on those
crutches," she says.

Olive and I get out.

We make it to the front gate.

The rain comes down harder.

I try to hurry.

My left crutch slips.

I fall and hit the ground.

Olive bends down to help me.

I push her arm away and tell her

to leave me alone.

She begins to cry.

It's all because of Doyle.

A.P. ENGLISH. I get to the classroom.

I hate walking on crutches. And I'm still wet from falling in the water.

Mr. Zimmer clicks on his computer and puts a test question on the screen.

"This is another essay like you'll have on the Advanced Placement test," he says. "You get forty minutes."

The question asks us to discuss a poem by Sir Philip Sidney.

I read the words. But my mind goes blank when I try to figure out what the poem means.

All I can think about is my knee.

Track season is over for me.

I won't be going to Munson State next year.

And it's all Doyle's fault.

PASSING PERIOD. I walk down the hall on my crutches.

It's time to go to peer tutoring.

But the closer I get, the madder I get.

I turn the corner and go to the health office.

I'll tell the nurse my knee is really hurting.

I don't want to be around Doyle.

LUNCH. I get to our table and sit with Hector and Vincent.

Doyle and Olive walk by. They're holding hands.

I can't stand it.

"Perry, what are you so mad about?" Hector asks.

"You look like you're going to explode," Vincent says.

I'm sick of what Doyle did to me.

I get ready to tell them what happened, that Doyle stole from our porch, that he was homeless, and that his mom is in jail.

But I remember the beaten look on Doyle's face when he was arrested.

And I remember the grateful look on his face when he thanked me for helping him.

"Are you okay?" Hector asks.

"Everything is fine," I say. "Sometimes, I just need to think about things."

17 STANDING UP

MONDAY MORNING. Peer tutoring. I
enter the study hall and sit at the
table with Doyle.

Something is wrong.

He has a look on his face like
he's been slammed again.

"Doyle, what happened?" I ask.

"I heard Ms. Jensen talking on
the phone to my social worker last
night. I might get sent to live with
another foster family."

"What for?"

"I don't know," he says. "But I

want to stay with the Jensens."

"Do you think you could have heard it wrong?"

"Maybe," he says. "But I do know this. I could get moved at any time."

I wish I knew what to say.

Things are always going wrong for him.

Mr. Rubio comes to the front. It looks like he's going to give another one of his speeches.

"Report card grades come out in two weeks," he says. "I know some of you are having a tough time. It's easy to get down on yourself, but don't give up. Make up your mind that you will stand up and keep trying."

I agree with what Mr. Rubio says about standing up.

But I'm tired of Doyle getting knocked down all the time.

It's not fair.

LOCKER ROOM. Period six. I knock on the door of the P.E. office.

Coach Quinty waves me in. "Perry, what can I do for you?"

"I have a friend who's a tenth grader. He's always wanted to run track. But his grades have been bad. I work with him in peer tutoring, and his grades are coming up. Is there any way he could run with the track team during practice?"

"What's his name?" Coach Quinty asks.

"Doyle Kemp. He's had a lot of tough breaks in his life. He needs somebody to give him a chance."

"Tell him to come and see me,"

Coach Quinty says. "If he can get a
C or higher in every class on the
next report card, he can run with us
during practice."

I know I'm smiling when I leave
the locker room.

For once, something is going to
go right for Doyle.

AFTER SCHOOL. Library. Doyle sits at
a computer when I get there.

I take the empty seat next to
him.

"Perry, that's a tough break
about your knee," Doyle says. "Olive
told me you have to get surgery."

"It's okay," I say. "The main
thing is that I'll be running next
year."

He gets onto the Khan Academy and
starts the first lesson.

It's hard for him, so he has to do it a second time.

But when he takes the test, he gets everything right.

"You remind me of what Mr. Rubio told us today," I say.

"What's that?" he asks.

"You get knocked down. But you keep standing up."

"Look at you with your knee," Doyle says. "Maybe you're doing the same thing."

He begins the next lesson.

Math has always been his worst subject.

But he's standing up now.

18 TWO WEEKS LATER

FRIDAY MORNING. Edison High School.
I walk through the front gate.

My knee hurts, so I still have to
use crutches.

The surgery is next week. It's
hard not to worry.

Dr. Thurman said it might be more
than just a torn meniscus. She might
have to do a reconstruction.

If that happens, my chances of
running track next year are not very
good.

PEER TUTORING. I enter the study hall and sit next to Doyle.

It's a big day for him. Report card grades come online at seven o'clock tonight.

"Are you ready to start running with the track team on Monday?" I ask.

"Not quite," he says. "I still have a D in math."

"Did you talk to Mr. Braden?"

"I saw him this morning. I have to pass two more tests on the Khan Academy by five o'clock tonight."

It worries me to hear him say that.

Mr. Braden loves to give D's.

AFTER SCHOOL. Library. Doyle is already working on the Khan Academy when I get there.

I sit in the chair next to him and watch as he works.

The first lesson is hard. He fails the test.

But he does the lesson again and passes the test a second time.

He begins the next lesson. There's only an hour left.

Then it happens.

The lights go off. The computers shut down.

We wait for the power to come back on.

Nothing.

I open my backpack and pull out my laptop.

"Doyle," I say. "Take this and run home. Get the lesson done and take the test. I know you can do it."

HOME. It's after five o'clock. I sit
at the kitchen table working on my
calculus.

It's hard not to worry about
Doyle.

My phone buzzes. It's a text from
him.

Finished test
Passed
Start track on Monday

It's the best news I've had in a
long time.

19   ONE YEAR LATER

THURSDAY AFTERNOON. Edison High has a track meet against Hamilton today.

I pay at the gate and enter the stadium. I'm here to watch Doyle.

Hector and Vincent sit by the announcer's booth. I take a seat next to them.

They both went away to college. I guess they're back for a visit.

"Perry, how are things at Raymond State?" Hector asks.

"Not bad," I say. "The classes are hard. But I'm doing okay."

"What about your knee?" Vincent asks.

"I'm running full speed again. I have a chance to go to the league finals in the 3200 meters."

The next race for Edison is the 100 meters. Doyle goes to the line and puts his feet in the blocks.

It's hard not to be nervous for him.

Bam!

The runners take off. Doyle starts slow. But he gains speed and comes in fourth place.

Doyle's next event is the hurdles. He gets fifth place.

He takes third place in the 200 meters.

It gives me a good feeling to watch him. He's come a long way.

LATER. I wait outside the locker
room. Doyle comes out. We shake
hands.

"Nice job," I say. "You looked
good out there."

"Thanks," he says. "My classes
are also good. I have a B in math
and an A in history."

"Are you still with the Jensens?"

"Yep," he says. "It's working
out."

Olive comes up and they hug. I
leave them alone and take a walk
around the campus.

It makes me feel good to know
that Doyle is okay.

I'm glad I was there to help him.

HOME. After dinner. Mom and I sit at
the kitchen table.

I work on an essay for American

Literature.

Mom grades papers for her seventh-grade English class.

"Do you ever get tired of checking papers?" I ask.

"I get tired of it every day," she says. "But I do it to see if the kids are learning."

I think about Doyle and what he's gone through. "I haven't said anything before. But I've been thinking about going into teaching."

"It's been great for me," Mom says. "But it's a lot of work. You also have to learn to see the other side of things."

"What do you mean?"

"When Doyle took that stuff off our porch, there was a reason for it," Mom says. "You saw the other side of things and figured out what

was going on with him. That's why
you were able to help him."

I never thought of it that way.
When I took peer tutoring, all I
cared about was getting an A.

But it wasn't the grade that was
important.

It was about Doyle getting
better.

20 DIDN'T GET

SUNDAY AFTERNOON. It's nice to have the house to myself.

And it's raining, so I don't have to do the yardwork.

I take another sip of coffee and look out the kitchen window.

I feel good about our track meet yesterday. My time was fast enough to make the league finals.

My grades are also strong. And I signed up for the teacher education program.

Next year, I'll volunteer as a

teacher assistant at a middle
school.

After I get my English degree,
I'll take a year of education
courses and do student teaching.

A delivery guy pulls up and
brings a box to our porch.

I put down my coffee and go to
the front door to get it.

It's something that Mom ordered.
I wonder if it's books.

EIGHT O'CLOCK. Dad makes his video
call. He's in Denver tonight.

First, he talks to Olive and Mom.
After that, it's my turn.

"Perry, Olive told me that Doyle
made the honor roll," Dad says. "Did
you know that?"

"I saw him after the track meet
on Thursday. But he didn't say

anything about the honor roll."

"You should feel good about what you did last year," Dad says. "You helped him a lot."

I think back to last year at this time.

My knee was torn up. I had to recover from surgery. And I didn't know if I would ever run track again.

But everything turned out okay.

My knee is fine.

Doyle is fine.

And we didn't get porched today.

ACKNOWLEDGMENTS

I would like to express my sincere gratitude to all of the people who gave me feedback while I was writing this book.

COFFEE HOUSE WRITERS GROUP: Paul Bello, Tracey Burke, Nicholas Chiazza, Nick Cruz, Sukie Fogg, Clyde Fugami, Lyndsey Getty, Samantha Hancox-Li, Richard Havenick, Steve Hovland, Vuthy Huot, Alex Khansa, Darian Lane, John Lowell, Ani Minisian, Colleen Nederlof, Jen Nelson, Viet Nguyen, Jean Pliska, Jared Reed, Amira Resnick, Ray Upton, Emily Wilder, R.P. Win, Dennis Wolverton, Mark Yang, Kurt, and Min.

SOCIETY OF CHILDREN'S BOOK WRITERS AND ILLUSTRATORS: Tim Burke, Lisa Gold, Nicole Green, Carlene Griffith, Karena Hamilton, Chris Jelbert, Jodi Rizzotto, Esther Tenenbaum, and Ann Worthington.

WRITERS INK: Tim Burke, Emily Heebner, Niki House, Teri Vitters, and Eric Young.

Thank you, Pam Sheppard, for your advice on creating this series.

Thank you, Laura Perkins, for your feedback and careful editing.

Thank you, Ron Connor and Kevin Gilbert, for your expertise and technical assistance.

Thank you, Betty Jean, for your
patience, your wisdom, your
suggestions, and for being my wife.

ABOUT THE AUTHOR

My dream of becoming a writer started at Whitworth College. I was lucky to have a teacher, Dr. Tammy Reid, who believed in me and encouraged me. After college, I began a career as an educator, teaching reading and English at a junior high school in Los Angeles. I went on to earn a doctorate in education. I also served as the principal of three high schools. One of the most important things I have learned as an educator, is that every student can achieve success. Set your sights high, work hard, and strive to be the best that you can be.

FINDING FORWARD BOOKS

At Finding Forward Books, we publish easy-to-read novels with positive life lessons that show teens overcoming challenges in their lives. Our goal is to help students improve their reading skills, develop positive attitudes, and increase their success in school.

The books are suitable for all students, including English Learners and those with learning disabilities. Lexile measures range from 390 to 560.

The books have been praised in *Kirkus Reviews*, *Publishers Weekly BookLife Reviews*, *Foreword Clarion Reviews*, and *BlueInk Reviews*.

ADDITIONAL TITLES

TAKEN AWAY. A teen learns to cope after his dad is sent to prison.

NO PLACE TO HIDE. A discouraged teen improves his reading skills.

NEVER WANTED. A neglected teen is placed in a foster home.

ALL ALONE. A teen learns to deal with his mom's alcoholism.

KNOCKED DOWN. A football player learns the importance of honesty.

OVERSPRAY. A teen must cope with feelings of grief after his father dies.

BLUE WALL. A troubled teen battles
back from depression.

LETTERZ. A teen struggling with
dyslexia learns how to succeed in
school.

CANS. A teen who dreams of attending
college struggles against poverty.

FINDING HOME. A homeless teen
strives to build a better life for
himself.

www.ingramcontent.com/pod-product-compliance
Lightning Source LLC
Chambersburg PA
CBHW030819200726

48288CB00004B/1304